P9-BYE-683

Sheila Says We're Weird

Ruth Ann Smalley

Illustrated by Jennifer Emery

TILBURY HOUSE, PUBLISHERS • GARDINER, MAINE

Sheila lives next door. She's friends with my little sister, Tina. Sheila asks lots of questions.

Sheila hangs over the back fence when we peg clothes on the line.

"Why don't you drop those in the dryer? Did it break?" Sheila asks.

"This is our solar dryer, Sheila. The clothes get dry without using any electricity."

"That's weird," Sheila says.

Sheila watches us plant our garden in the spring.

"Why don't you just have a regular yard?" Sheila asks.

"We like growing flowers and food. The garden helps feed us and the bees."

"That's weird," Sheila says.

Sheila pokes her head out her
porch window when we use our rotary mower to cut her grass.
"Why don't you use a real lawn mower?" she asks.
"This *is* a real mower. It cuts the grass using people power—
no noise, no smelly fumes!"

"That's weird," Sheila says.

In the summer, Sheila skips in through our screen door and says, "Why don't you turn on the air conditioner?"

"The ceiling fan keeps us cool. Air conditioners gobble up electricity. Fans only sip a little."

"That's weird," Sheila says.

Sheila sees Mom pulling the tea bags out of the big jar of sun tea brewing on the windowsill.

"Why don't you toss those tea bags in the trash can?" Sheila asks.

"They make great worm food," Mom says, putting them in the worm bin.

"That's really, really weird," Sheila says.

In the fall, we rake leaves and put them on our garden.

"Why don't you stuff 'em in a bag, and stick 'em on the curb?" Sheila asks.

"We like to make mulch. It protects the plants in winter, and helps them sprout in spring."

"That's weird," Sheila says.

On Saturdays, we go to the farmer's market.
We bring home baskets of apples, cheese, and eggs.
Sheila spies us and scooters over.

"Why don't you get your groceries from the store?"
she asks.

"We like local food. It's fresher and tastes better
when it comes from nearby farmers. And it doesn't
use so much energy to get to us."

"That's weird," Sheila says.

In the winter, when Sheila sees Dad putting a log in the wood stove, she says, "Why don't you just turn up the heat?"

"We can warm up around the fire. That way, we don't waste heat on empty rooms."

"That's weird," Sheila says.

W hen we're chopping up vegetables to make a big pot of soup, Sheila says, "Why don't you just open a can of soup and put it in the microwave?"

"We like homemade food. It's even more delicious when we make it from scratch."

"That's weird," Sheila says.

Sheila also wants to know why we:

ride our bikes to the library,

repair our clothes,

use cloth napkins,

and carry our own water
bottles when we go out.

B ut I notice that:
Sheila loves to pick and eat the strawberries
and cherry tomatoes in our garden.

And Sheila is so happy to take home bouquets of flowers.

And Sheila never misses a chance to play dolls
with Tina in front of the fire on chilly days.

And Sheila gets excited about her turn to shake the pan when we make popcorn on the wood stove.

And Sheila is always ready for a bowl of soup—and maybe a second bowl, too.

So, Sheila says we're weird—but I think she likes us a lot.

TILBURY HOUSE, PUBLISHERS

103 Brunswick Avenue, Gardiner, Maine 04345

800–582–1899 · www.tilburyhouse.com

First hardcover edition: July 2011 · 10 9 8 7 6 5 4 3 2 1

Text copyright © 2011 by Ruth Ann Smalley

Illustrations copyright © 2011 by Jennifer Emery

All Rights Reserved. No part of this publication may be reproduced or transmitted in any form or by any means, electronic or mechanical, including photocopy, recording, or any information storage or retrieval system, without permission in writing from the publisher.

Dedications:

For Mom, Dad, and John, for helping me dare to be weird. —RAS

For my friend and fellow artist, Franc Robles. —JE

Library of Congress Cataloging-in-Publication Data

Smalley, Ruth Ann.

Sheila says we're weird / Ruth Ann Smalley ; illustrated by Jennifer Emery. — 1st hardcover ed.

p. cm.

Summary: Sheila comments on her neighbors' energy-saving habits, like using a wood stove in the winter and drying clothes on a clothesline instead of in the dryer, but she likes their home-grown fruits and vegetables and enjoys making popcorn on the wood stove with them.

ISBN 978-0-88448-326-7 (hardcover : alk. paper)

[1. Energy conservation—Fiction. 2. Neighbors—Fiction.] I. Emery, Jennifer, ill. II. Title. III. Title: Sheila says we're weird.

PZ7.S639142Sh 2011

[E]—dc22

2010047972

Designed by Geraldine Millham, Westport, Massachusetts

Printed and bound by Sung In Printing Ltd., Dang Jung-Dong 242-2, GungPo-si, Kyunggi-do, Korea; April 2011.